WORKING MUMMIES

WRITTEN BY
Joan Horton

ILLUSTRATED BY
Drazen Kozjan

FARRAR

STRAUS

GIROUX

New York

Text copyright © 2012 by Joan Horton
Pictures copyright © 2012 by Drazen Kozjan
All rights reserved
Distributed in Canada by D&M Publishers, Inc.
Color separations by Embassy Graphics
Printed in China by South China Printing Co. Ltd., Dongguan City, Guangdong Province
Designed by Roberta Pressel
First edition, 2012
10 9 8 7 6 5 4 3 2 1

mackids.com

Library of Congress Cataloging-in-Publication Data
Horton, Joan.
     Working mummies / Joan Horton ; pictures by Drazen Kozjan. — 1st ed.
          p.   cm.
     Summary: Illustrations and rhyming text introduce the many careers and professions of
mummies, such as real estate agents selling haunted houses and dentists filing vampires' fangs.
     ISBN: 978-0-374-38524-8
     [1. Stories in rhyme.   2. Occupations—Fiction.   3. Mummies—Fiction.   4. Monsters—Fiction.
5. Mothers—Fiction.]   I. Kozjan, Drazen, ill.   II. Title.

PZ8.3.H78753Wor 2012
[E]—dc23

                                                                                                      2011018296

For my great-uncle Albert —J.H.

For hardworking mummies Lydia, Heather, Susan,
and especially my Mummy and Pat —D.K.

Mummies work at different jobs—
In buildings short and tall,
In diners, schools, and hospitals
And at the local mall.

Some mummies work in pet stores
Selling lizards, toads, and bats
While a manicurist mummy
Sharpens claws for yowling cats.

SKROGS ON SALE

Then doses them with coffin syrup

To soothe their frightful groans.

Wanda's mum's a waitress.
She says, "*Bone appétit!*"
When serving hungry skeletons
Big bowls of Scream of Wheat.

A writer mummy works at home.
She isn't a commuter.
She conjures spells for witches
On her personal computer.

Other mums sell houses.
They're not the least bit daunted
By buyers who insist upon
Old dwellings that are haunted.

A beautician mummy's busy
When the moon is full and bright.
She curls the hair on werewolves
So they won't look such a fright.

JETWOLF-O-DRY

Hilda's mum's a teacher.
Her smile becomes a frown
Whenever screaming goblins
Refuse to quiet down.

Mummies who are caterers
Cook up a tasty feast
Of ribs and baby bat wings
For one hundred drooling beasts.

This mummy's a librarian.
She has a great selection
Of rare and wiggly book worms
In her specimen collection.

Igor's mum's a dentist.
She uses extra care
When filing fangs of vampires
As they lie back in her chair.

Some mummies work the graveyard shift
To turn out by the dozens
Replacement parts for Frankenstein
And all his monster cousins.

But no matter where the mummies work—
In diners, stores, or schools—
They can't unwind until they're home . . .

To hug their boys and ghouls.